Dear Abi

When the lady who wrote this book knew it
for your birthday I was buying it, she wanted to
wish you happy birthday too. So she did!

To Abi
Happy 5th. Birthday.
Eileen Townend

and so do I. Have a Happy Birthday.

Love

Carol

The Fabulous Life of Honey Furrari

The Picnic

My special thanks to Sara for her invaluable help with this book.

Published by Gooseworks

Printed and bound in China

www.hxbookprinting.com

ISBN - 978-0-9567511-0-2

$\mathcal{W}$elcome to my world. My name is Honey Furrari and since you are reading this, I'm about to invite you on an exciting adventure. If you don't know already, I'm a dog. "Dog", I dislike that word. "Canine", now that sounds far more intelligent. I live in the beautiful village of Little Snoring and yes, it may look like your typical sleepy English village, but there are lots of magical things that happen when everyone is asleep.

*T*his is my story. I'm two years old, well, in dog years that makes me quite the teenager. My owner is fabulous, but she knows nothing about my secret double life, and just so that you know, she likes to be called Mummy. I was born on a cold Winter's day. The snow had settled elegantly on the rooftop of the thatched cottage where I lay with my canine mother Matilde and my brothers and sisters by the warm fire. Matilde gently licked the white stripe across my back three times, and that's when the magic began......

2

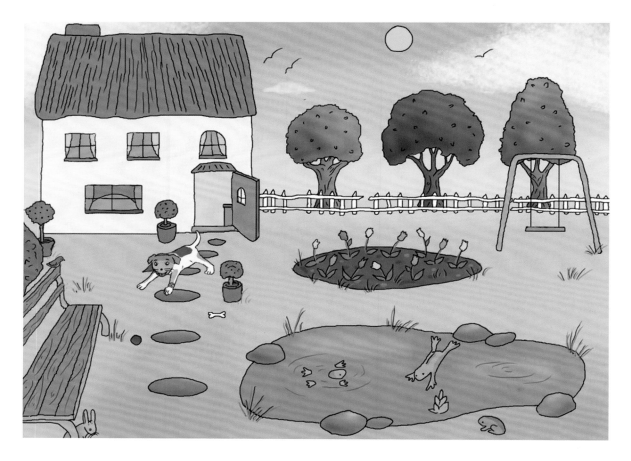

$\mathcal{L}$et me invite you into my home. If you follow me out of the back door you can see my enchanting garden and lying on the grass is my favourite red ball, which I do enjoy playing a good game of Fetch with. Sometimes when I'm not completely concentrating it will roll into the pond where the slippery, slimy frogs live. I put on a brave face, however, take a deep breath and jump in after it and when I emerge I look very bedraggled, but I smile and wag my tail for Mummy.

4

*J*ust now I'm feeling quite sleepy after all that running about, so let's go upstairs and I'll show you where my bed is. Mummy is turning out the lights down below and the stairs creak as she walks upon them with a cup of green tea in her hand. As she strokes me goodnight, I curl up on my soft bed and listen as she tells me about her day. Just before I close my eyes, I lick my magic stripe three times and know that this will send me into a different world.

$\mathcal{M}$y mind starts to drift away and before I know it I am in a heavy sleep. All Mummy can hear is my gentle snoring, which is my only flaw! I begin to feel as though I am floating, and then before I know it I am flying through the sky and through beautiful pink candy floss clouds. Suddenly I feel myself falling, falling and take a quick bite from the delicious tasting cloud before I touch the ground. As I shake myself to recover from the fall, to my surprise I find myself behind the wheel of a brand new convertible sports car.

$\mathcal{N}$ow I am on the open road, my fur blowing in the wind and wearing a pair of glamourous sunglasses which I found in the glove compartment. I turn up the radio, look in the rear view mirror and can see a brown wicker hamper on the back seat, with a note attached to it reading, "HEAD TO THE WOODS". Driving off in that direction and hoping to meet up with my furry friends, I do wonder who the note can be from. I have an uneasy feeling that something is not quite right.

$\mathcal{A}$rriving at my destination, I park the shiny red car and, grabbing the hamper between my teeth, jog to my special spot. I begin to lay out the picnic onto a wide wooden log in a clearing and wonder, "Where is everyone?" Suddenly there is a loud screech, a hefty thump, and Edgar the owl is falling from the sky, his feathers flying everywhere. He really is in quite a state. "Quick Honey," he squawks breathlessly. "Cyril the Squirrel has fallen into the river and can't get out!"

$\mathcal{E}$dgar is flapping his wings in a panic as he follows behind me, and there all of a sudden we can see Cyril clinging to a broken branch. He looks so scared! Edwina the Weasel is hanging from a tree, trying to use her tail as a rope to reach him. My first thought is to get Cyril out safely but my second is, "I bet Boris the Panther is behind this".

Straight away I jump into the river and swim towards Cyril, but as soon as I get close the current pushes me back. After several attempts to get near him and Cyril gasping, "Oh save me Honey please, save me!" I decide some urgent action is needed and, soaked to the skin, I run back to the car barking "Back in a jiffy!"

I put my paw down hard on the accelerator and drive straight back through the wood. Twigs are hitting the window and leaves are falling onto my coat. At the clearing I reverse towards the river bank, hoping to find a strong rope to attach to the car in order to rescue Cyril. When I look into the car boot no rope is to be found. Edgar is still flapping over me in a total fluster. Suddenly I hear a hissing sound and there on the ground is Frazzle, a long yellow and green snake, his scales glittering in the sunlight. "Wouldsss you likesss somesss helpsss?" he hisses.

Frazzle's face looks sincere, but I know if I look into his hypnotic eyes it will be a different story. "Is this a trap?" I think, knowing that Boris the Panther is his best friend, "or does he really want to help?" All I can hear is Cyril screaming, so I need any help I can get. "Yes!" I bark and Frazzle attaches himself to the back of the car with his body dangling in the river.

Frazzle's tail is splashing to and fro in the water, and Cyril is trying his hardest to grab on to it. Every time his paws reach out for the tail, they slide off again, so Frazzle finally curves his body into a hook shape, Cyril clings on to it and with a big tug from the car he shoots right out of the river. Edwina and Edgar rush over to comfort Cyril and I jump out of the car to thank Frazzle for his help. Maybe he isn't as bad as I thought.....but then I catch sight of a large dark shape moving silently in the shadows.

"*T*hank you," I say and for the first time I look into Frazzle's eyes and they start to spin, his scarlet pupils holding my attention. For a few moments it's fascinating, then a cold shudder comes over me. "You owesss me," he hisses, his tail curling as he slithers away into the grass and out of sight.

We all gather around the picnic log, where previously I had set out lunch and Cyril tells the story of how he fell, but as I listen to his account it doesn't all make sense. "How would such a nimble mover as Cyril have fallen in while playing? Wasn't it strange that Frazzle was there at the very time we needed help?" I thought. As the squirrel ends his story he gives me a distressed look, indicating that he doesn't want to upset the others with the truth, but I believe that Boris pushed him!

After we have eaten our delicious lunch and Cyril is nicely dry and warm again, we pack away the picnic. I give Edwina and Cyril a long embrace goodbye, for with my magical dreams I'm never sure when we will next meet. Edgar flies over to me and pecks my cheek, making me blush! Once Cyril has promised never to juggle his acorns over the river again, I smile, bark and wag my tail, returning to my sports car. As I drive off towards the West I turn my head. Is that a dark shadow I can see still moving in the trees?

I look into the sky and the sun is setting in a beautiful pink and orange glow. As I drive faster the car starts to lift off the ground. I accelerate and fly higher and higher into the air. When I turn on my headlights the car sparkles and glitters.....my body feels as if I am going through a whirlwind, my eyes are shut tight.

When I open my eyes again I am lying on my bed at home and can see Mummy awaking from her sleep too. The sun has risen and I can hear the cockerel crowing. It's going to be another beautiful day.

*E*xcuse me a moment while I stretch myself to wake up completely...that's better, now we can go downstairs for breakfast. When I walk past the great mirror I see my reflection and take a moment to ponder on last night, but I really am back in the world of Little Snoring and so now it will be all about walks in the countyrside and being pampered!

As Mummy and I sit outside in the garden and I watch her eating her slice of toast spread lightly with marmalade, she throws my red ball and I run to collect it. Racing back with the ball in my mouth, I roll it on the ground to her so that she can throw it again. As she bends down to pick it up her morning newspaper falls from her lap. The headline reads "Black Panther Escapes From Local Zoo"....................

Perhaps my dreams are becoming a reality....